TO LUKE
HAPPY READING!

Mark Collins

Luke,
    We met the author/illustrator and
he signed this one especially for you!
                Love, Aunt Sylvia
                        and
Christmas, 2019   Uncle John

TO LUKE

HAPPY READING

GRANDMA STINKS!

STORY AND PICTURES BY
MARK C. COLLINS

For Mindy and Austin – my greatest inspirations.

Mom said Grandma was
coming to live with us.
She would travel
a long way to get here.
I couldn't wait to see her!

I was so happy
when Grandma arrived.
She gave me a big hug.

That's when I noticed…

GRANDMA STINKS!

I held my breath
when Grandma told me
about her trip.

When Grandma headed into the bathroom, I asked Mom, "Have you noticed? **GRANDMA STINKS!**"

Mom said I should be nice. "Go help Grandma settle in."

I carried Grandma's bags
to the guest room.

While Grandma unpacked,
I ran to Dad.
"Dad, have you noticed?
GRANDMA STINKS!"

He agreed, then told me to
prepare a bath for Grandma.
"Great idea, Dad!"

After filling the tub with warm water
and sweet-smelling bath oils,
I ran to Grandma's room.

"Grandma, I made a nice, warm
bath for you to relax in!"

I ran to the kitchen, made the tea,
then hurried back with her cup.

Grandma thanked me, took off
her shoes, and put her feet up.

I ran to the pantry to get an
air freshener for Grandma's room.

It didn't help.

All my running around helping
Grandma made me sweaty.

Grandma turned to me and
whispered, "You stink, Dearie."

Just then, Mom called us for dinner.

I washed up and
took my seat at the table.
Grandma sat next to me.

The food looked really tasty,
but I could barely eat, because…

GRANDMA STINKS!

After dinner, Mom asked me to
take Grandma for a walk.
I imagined the fresh air would
make Grandma smell better.

"Great idea, Mom!"

While we walked, it started to rain.
PERFECT...

or so I thought.

When we got home, we were
soaking wet, and Grandma
was stinkier than ever.

Back inside, Grandma
mistakenly dried herself
with MY towel!

Now my towel stinks
like Grandma.

I changed into fresh, dry clothes.

I was happy to see
Grandma did too.

Grandma asked me to fetch a
package from one of her bags.
I ran to her room, then
returned with the package.

"Open it, Dearie. It's for you."
Inside was a beautiful doll
that looked like me!
"Thank you, Grandma!"

While I played with my new doll,
Grandma brushed my hair
and added colorful ribbons.

Later, Grandma gave me
an old photo album.

She sat with me while
I turned the pages.

Grandma told me about her life
in the old pictures, and I noticed
she looked just like me
when she was a little girl!

She told me about Grandpa, and
that he had died many years ago.

Then she leaned in and whispered,
"I love you, Emma."
Of course I covered my nose,
because…

well, **you** know why.

At bedtime, I said goodnight to Mom and Dad, then Grandma tucked me in.

She read a bedtime story from a book in her native language.

I didn't understand, but it sounded so beautiful. I drifted off to sleep and dreamed of pretty things…

and Grandma.

Next morning, I awoke to
a wonderful smell.

I ran to the kitchen where Grandma
was happily serving breakfast.

Everything tasted so good!

Then I remembered...

GRANDMA STINKS!

But it no longer bothered me!
I didn't have to hold my breath.

That's when I knew it doesn't matter that Grandma stinks. She loves me, and I love her... **just the way she is!**

The
End

About The Author

I began drawing at the age of two, and have wanted to be an artist for as long as I can remember. After graduating from art school, I went through almost two decades as a graphic designer before switching to illustration solely, and since 2001 I've illustrated for textbooks, magazines, packaging, and other authors' books.

Through the course of my life, I've dabbled in poetry, song writing, short stories, and recently took up writing children's books. This is an area where I can combine my writing, design, and illustration skills into fun, colorful works for kids (and adults).

Mark Collins

Mark C. Collins (illustrator) is represented by DEBORAH WOLFE, LTD, and his work can be seen on the web at **IllustrationOnline.com**.

Other books by Mark C. Collins - available on Amazon.com
- **Ben's Day**
- **Meet The Bugs!**
- **Harry's Hair**

Website: **markcollinsillustration.com**

 facebook.com/pages/Mark-Collins-Illustration/163120997136936

 pinterest.com/mcillustr8r

 twitter.com/KILLUSTR8R

Made in the
USA
Monee, IL